PUSH IT!

MARLA CONN

Rourke Educational Media
A Division of Carson Dellosa Education

rourkeeducationalmedia.com

Photo Glossary

button

crayon

lawn mower

swing

toy

wagon

High Frequency Words:
- a
- can
- push
- you

3

You can push a **button**.

button

You can push a **lawn mower.**

lawn mower

7

You can push a **wagon**.

wagon

You can push a **crayon**.

crayon

You can push a **swing**.

12

swing

You can push a **toy**.

toy

15

Activity

1. Name all of the things from the story that you can **PUSH**.
2. Find things from home or school and practice **PUSHING**.
3. Discuss the following questions-
    - What is motion?
    - What does something in motion look like?
    - What does it mean to **PUSH** an object?
    - Does how hard I **PUSH** it matter?
    - If I **PUSH** something, where does it go?
4. Write a sentence and draw a picture of something you can push.